THE SECRET EXPLORERS AND THE LOST WHALES

SJ King

CONTENTS

Chapter One
POND DIPPING

Connor dipped his net into the pond and scooped up a big clump of algae. Long green strands of the tiny plants trailed down. It looked like Connor had caught a watery monster. ***I guess I have***, he thought. After all, too much algae would block out the light, and the other plants in the pond would die.

Connor had spent the morning clearing

up the water. The pond was at the end of his backyard, on the other side of the white picket fence. The leaves of the pecan trees gleamed in the warm Missouri sunshine.

Connor dropped the algae onto the bank. He was about to scoop out another clump, when he noticed something wriggling inside the net. A tadpole!

"Hey, there!" said Connor. "Are you going to grow into a bullfrog? Or maybe a leopard frog?" Gently, he lowered the net so the tadpole could escape. He watched it swim away, kicking its tiny back legs. It joined a large group of tadpoles beside some reeds.

Hold on, Connor thought. ***They're hanging out in a shoal... Those probably aren't frog tadpoles—I think they're toads!***

Connor loved everything about the water. His mom thought he would be a marine biologist when he grew up and study the plants and animals in the sea.

"We'll have to take a vacation to the coast one day," Mom had said at breakfast. "Wouldn't it be amazing to see the ocean?"

Connor touched the compass badge on his chest. His mom didn't know that Connor had seen lots of oceans already...

When he'd scooped out the last gloopy blob of algae, Connor propped his net against the wooden fence. It was hot now. The sunshine shimmered on the wheat fields that surrounded his house. Connor made his way indoors.

He washed his hands at the kitchen sink, then went to the pantry to get himself a granola bar. There was a postcard tacked to the pantry door. It said, "I Love Missouri Science Fair!" Connor had won first prize in the competition for growing coral in a tank.

As he reached for the door handle, he stopped in surprise.

A glowing shape had appeared next to the postcard.

It was a circle with a needle in the center. Around the outside were the letters N, S, E, and W.

A compass!

A compass that matched the badge on Connor's T-shirt...

Connor grinned. ***The Secret Explorers have a new mission!*** he thought.

Excitement tingled through him as he stepped through the door. The shelves of food were gone, and instead there was a dazzling white light. Connor's heart thudded. Wind whipped against his face, as if he were traveling really fast...

A moment later, the light faded. Connor was standing in a large, familiar room. Light from the rows of computer screens flickered on the black stone walls. Objects stood on display in glass cabinets, just like in a museum. There were dinosaur fossils, meteorites from space, and shells from the bottom of the ocean. On the floor was a huge map of the world. The domed ceiling showed the stars and the Milky Way. Connor was back in the Exploration Station!

"Connor—here!" he said.

Near the computers was a cluster of comfy chairs. A girl with short dark hair jumped up from one of them. A compass badge just like Connor's was pinned to her soccer jersey.

"Hey, Tamiko!" said Connor. He noticed her cool Stegosaurus necklace—Tamiko's specialty subject was dinosaurs.

"Hi!" Tamiko said. "Look—here come the others!"

The rest of the Secret Explorers began to hurry through the glowing doorway. A tall, grinning girl gave a salute, just like she always did. "Leah—here!" she called. Leah knew everything about plants and animals.

Next came Kiki, who loved machines and technology. She wore glasses and pajamas, and her hair was still ruffled from sleep.

"Kiki—here!"

"Ollie—here!" said a red-haired boy in a rain forest T-shirt.

The rest of the team called out their names. There was Roshni, who wanted to be an astronaut, Gustavo who loved history, and Cheng who knew everything about rocks and volcanoes.

The roll call was complete. Connor was buzzing with excitement—now they would be given their mission! Everyone took their usual place around the map on the floor.

Sure enough, a circle of light glimmered on part of the map. Connor recognized where it was right away—the South Pacific Ocean, to the east of Australia. The circle got bigger. It became the size of a TV screen. It showed a pod of whales diving through the water. They had long fins and white bellies.

"Humpback whales," said Connor.

But who would the Exploration Station choose for this adventure? It always picked the two members with the right skills and knowledge for the mission.

Connor looked down to see his compass badge glowing with light. "I'm in!" he cried. He was the club's marine expert, so that made sense. But who would be his teammate? Roshni's badge shimmered, lighting up her face.

"Cool!" Roshni said. "But my specialty is space. I wonder what that's got to do with humpback whales?"

"I guess we'll find out," said Connor. He gave her a high five. "The Exploration Station is never wrong!"

Kiki pressed a button on one of the computers. A vehicle with two seats rose up from the floor. "The Beagle, ready to go," Kiki said. The Beagle was named after a ship sailed by the famous scientist Charles Darwin. It looked like an old go-kart, with chipped paint and a crooked steering wheel.

But it's so much more than just a go-kart, Connor thought.

The other Secret Explorers took their places at the computers, ready to give Connor and Roshni any help they needed during their mission.

"Good luck!" called Cheng.

"Can't wait to hear all about it!" added Tamiko.

"Call us if you need anything!" said Kiki.

Connor and Roshni waved goodbye to their friends, then clambered into the Beagle. Connor gripped the steering wheel. "Ready?" he asked.

Roshni nodded. "Ready."

He leaned forward and pressed a button on the dashboard that said "START." The Beagle began to shake. The nuts and bolts shuddered as if they would pop out at any moment. There was a bright flash. The Beagle jerked forward, and Connor and Roshni were flung back against their seats. Suddenly, they were zooming through a tunnel of light.

Beneath them, the Beagle began to transform. The wheels slid away. A joystick replaced the steering wheel. Glass rose around them. "Maybe it's turning into a boat this time!" Connor cried, his voice trembling under the force.

There was a huge splash. Connor gazed out in wonder through a curved window. Blue water stretched as far as he could see.

Overhead flew a white tropic bird with long tail feathers.

"It's the Pacific Ocean!" he said.

Roshni pointed at a periscope sticking up through the glass ceiling of the cockpit.

"We're not in a boat," she said with a grin. "We're in a submarine!"

r Two

HE SEARCH HEATS UP

A dashboard rose up from the Beagle's floor. Panels popped open to reveal screens and switches. The change was complete and the Beagle bobbed peacefully on the water.

"Look at all these controls!" Connor said excitedly. "What do you think they do?"

Roshni grinned. "Let's find out."

Every time the Beagle changed to a new

vehicle, it took on new special features. Figuring out what everything did was half the fun.

Connor pointed out a round screen with glowing green lights. "This must be the sonar," he said. "It uses sound waves to measure distances underwater."

"I think this is for navigation," said Roshni, who was peering into a display. "There's us, look, and there's the seabed under us. It's like a satnav."

In the cupboards under the dashboard were energy bars, water bottles, and two wet suits with masks and oxygen tanks.

"We can go on a dive!" Connor said. "Wait until you see the coral up close. It's amazing. So many colors. And the fish come right up to you!"

"We'd better find the whales first," Roshni replied.

"For sure," Connor agreed.

They were here to help, he reminded himself. They didn't yet know what sort of help the whales needed, but the Exploration Station had sent them here for a reason.

Roshni turned her seat to face the sonar screen. "Why don't you drive and I'll work the instruments?"

"Cool!"

Connor gripped the joystick with one

hand and the depth control with the other. He slowly brought the Beagle down below the surface. Lapping water rose around the glass bubble.

Down in the green depths, everything was much quieter. Waves danced above them like a silver sheet. Light slanted down in faint rays. Soon, the only sound was the thrumming of the engines.

"See anything?" Connor asked.

Roshni peered into the murk. "Not yet," she said.

Connor took them deeper.

Roshni frowned at the sonar screen. "Still nothing."

"That's weird," Connor said. "I can't see any creatures at all down here. Not even a shrimp!"

The cabin suddenly became much darker. Something was blotting out all the light.

"Look!" Roshni pointed up. "Is that the whale pod?"

High above them passed a huge shadow.

"Could be," Connor said. "Let's take a look."

But as they drew close, Connor soon saw it wasn't the whales at all.

Hanging over them was an enormous cloud of bright red algae. It made the sea look like tomato soup. The algae covered the water for what looked like miles in every direction.

They surfaced in the middle of the stuff. Red liquid slid down the windows.

"It's like the surface of Mars," Roshni whispered in amazement.

"And about as much good for life," Connor said. "That's a red tide. Also known as an algal bloom."

Connor knew that this kind of algae was bad for marine life because it released poisons into the water. There was no sense in blaming the algae though. They fed on farm fertilizer that had been washed out to sea and grew so fast because climate change had warmed the oceans.

Human beings had caused this mess.

"No point looking for the whales here." He sighed. "They feed off these little critters called krill. Guess what a red tide does to krill?"

"Kills them?" Roshni guessed.

Connor nodded. "Let's keep moving."

He fired the engines. The Beagle churned

up the water and they plunged below the surface again. Connor was glad to leave that ugly red soup behind.

As they moved out of the algal bloom's shadow, the water began to clear. Little gleaming fish zipped past. Then came a pulsing jellyfish with tentacles like streamers. Connor smiled. This was more like it!

He steered them down toward the seabed. Roshni switched on the outside lights and gasped.

The beams lit up a wonderland of life. Before them lay brightly colored kelp beds, clumps of coral like heaps of treasure, and schools of glittering fish.

As they approached a bulging rock, it suddenly moved! The rock changed color and reached out with its striped tentacles. It snatched up a crab.

Roshni gave a yelp of surprise, then a delighted laugh. "It's an octopus!"

"A mimic octopus, and it's a beauty," said Connor. "They're camouflage experts."

"I noticed." Roshni grinned. "Hey, is that a shark? It looks like an alien."

Off in the distance, a pale gray shape was gliding along silently, looking for prey.

Its strange head was T-shaped, with eyes at the ends.

"Yep," said Connor. "A hammerhead."

They steered the Beagle carefully around the rocks and reefs, still searching for the whales. There was no sign. Once a hidden manta ray rose up from the seabed, sending clouds of sand everywhere. But there were still no whales.

"Maybe there's something on the sub that can help us," Roshni said, looking around. "Turbo boost..." She read out the labels under the buttons. "Grabbing arm... Hey, what about this sound scanner?"

"Go for it," Connor said.

Roshni pressed a switch. The cabin suddenly filled with the noises made by the different sea creatures outside. Crabs scuttled and clicked. A hammerhead shark thrashed its tail.

Then, from the dim distance, came an eerie, echoing sound. Connor froze. "Listen! That's them!"

They both held their breath. For almost a whole minute, there was only silence. Then they both heard it again, loud and clear.

Connor thought there was no other sound on Earth like the song of a humpback whale—a soaring, shivering, lonely call that somehow seemed to come from the far-off stars. His skin tingled.

"Wow," Roshni breathed.

"I know, right?" Connor pointed forward.

"They're definitely in that direction."

"Let's see if we can find them with the sonar!" Roshni said.

She pressed a button. Sure enough, the pod of whales popped up on the screen! They were swimming together over an underwater valley.

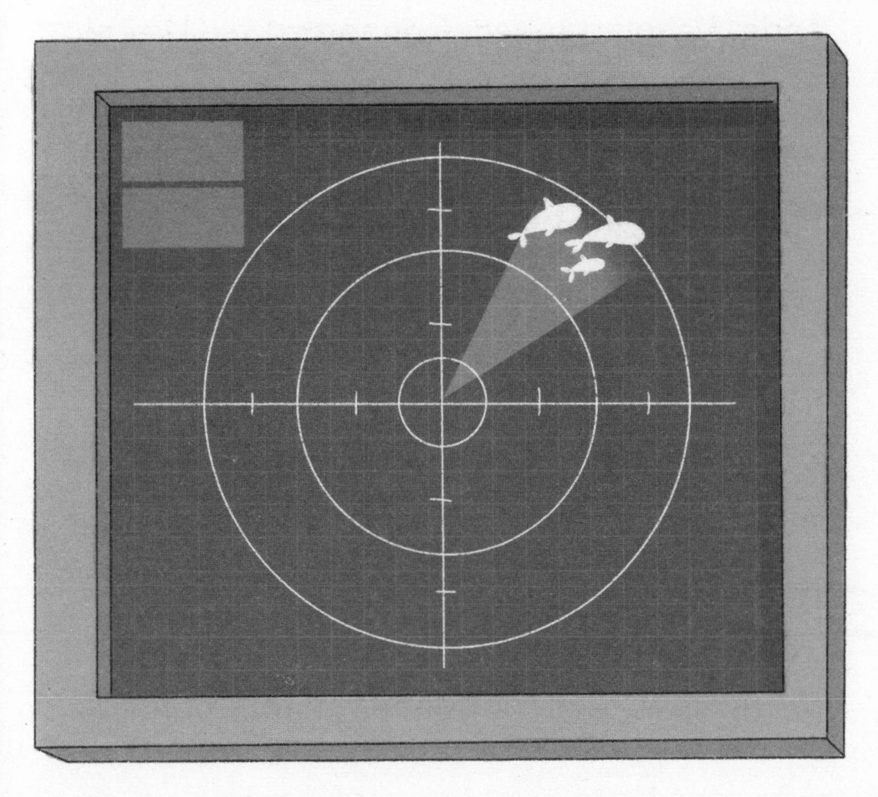

"We need to follow them!" Connor said.

Roshni's fingers danced over the controls. With a loud ping, a glowing green arrow appeared on the dashboard, pointing the way to the whales.

"Full speed ahead, Captain Connor!" she yelled.

"Aye, aye!" Connor growled and slammed the engines up to maximum thrust. They were flung back in their seats as the Beagle roared through the ocean like a torpedo.

It wasn't long before they caught sight of

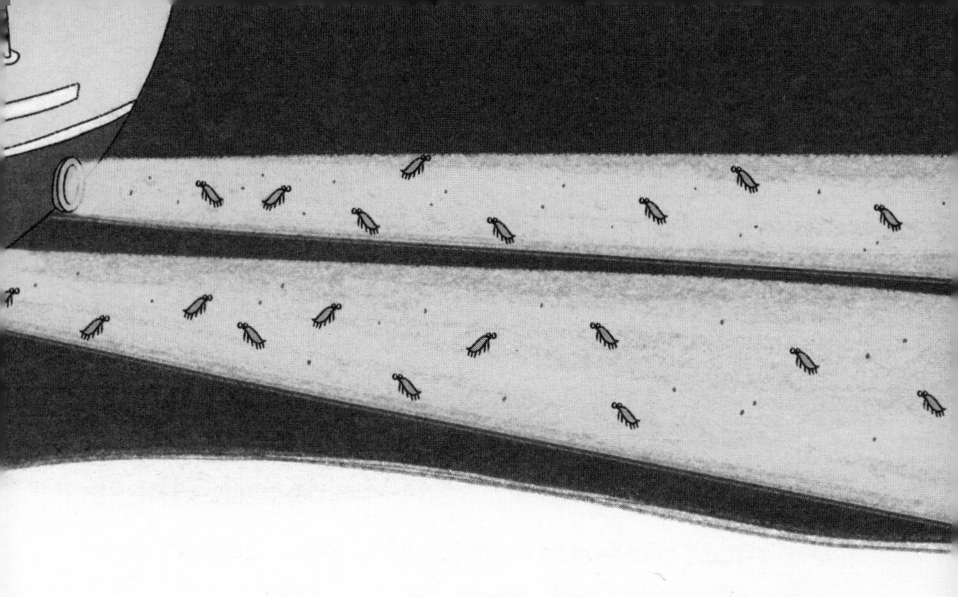

the same deep valley they'd seen with the sonar. Tiny creatures with lots of legs were swimming through the sub's headlights.

Krill!

Connor slowed the engines down. They had to be close.

Any moment now...

"There they are!" he said in an awed whisper.

The humpback whales were coming into view. One after another, their immense shapes emerged from the cloudy depths.

Connor looked on, his heart pounding, as their mighty tails beat a path through the ocean. How could something so enormous be so graceful?

"I hope the other Secret Explorers are watching right now," he said, "because this is the most awesome thing I've ever seen!"

Chapter Three

MAKE SOME NOISE

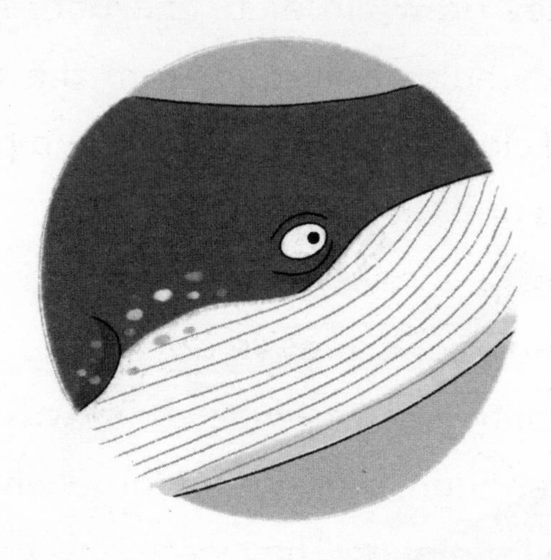

Now that he could see the humpback whales clearly, Connor was worried. They needed help, but what kind? He didn't like to think of these beautiful creatures being in danger.

"Can we get closer?" Roshni asked excitedly.

"Sure," Connor replied. "But not too close. We don't want to spook them."

He turned the engines down until they were coasting quietly through the water. As they drew closer to the pod, more and more whales emerged from the murk. He could clearly see the knobbly bumps on their heads and their wise little eyes.

Roshni's own eyes widened and she gasped. "Look, they've got *babies*!"

Connor looked where she was pointing. Sure enough, among the large whales were some little ones. They were only a few yards long, and each was swimming close to an adult whale. Those had to be their mothers.

"Calves," Connor said.

"Huh? Where?"

"That's what you call a baby whale. This mission just got even more important, Roshni."

Roshni nodded, her face serious. "We've got to protect these guys. So what's the danger? Predators?"

"I can't tell yet," Connor said. "But I know one thing. These whales give birth in Pacific waters, where it's warm. So now they must be migrating south to Antarctica. The water there is cold, but it's full of krill for them to eat."

The Beagle, which had been quiet until now, let out a sudden **BEEP!** Red lights flashed on the console.

Connor and Roshni stared at it.

Connor asked "What's up, Beagle? Did I get something wrong?"

BEEP! the Beagle repeated.

"Wait." Roshni held up a hand. "You said the whales were swimming south. But the sun's right in front of us right now. And the whales are swimming toward it. And it's nearly sunset, and the sun sets in the west. So that means..."

BLOO-BOOPOP, jabbered the Beagle encouragingly. It sounded like "keep talking."

"...the whales are swimming west, not south!" Roshni exclaimed.

Connor sat bolt upright in his seat. "You're right. They're swimming toward Australia, not Antarctica. The pod of whales is off course!"

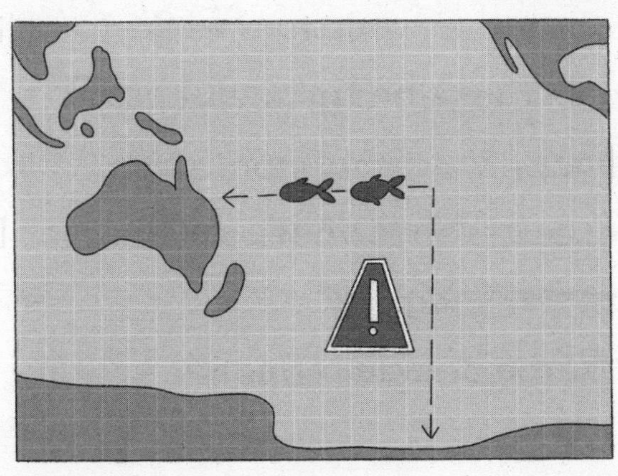

The Beagle made a triumphant ***DING!*** noise like someone ringing a bell.

"But how could the whales have gone the wrong way?" Roshni said. "They use the same migration route every year, don't they?"

Connor thought he knew what had happened. "Remember that red tide we saw? Maybe the whales didn't want to swim through that stuff. They might have gotten lost trying to avoid it."

They both looked out at the whales, who were all swimming powerfully in the wrong direction. Connor and Roshni understood now what their mission was—to get the whale pod back on track. But how?

"You're the marine expert, Connor," Roshni said. "What do we do?"

Connor thought hard. Those whales were huge, strong, and determined. Getting them

to change course wouldn't be easy. He tried to remember how other people had helped whales in the past.

"I read about a whale that was trapped in a harbor," he said. "It didn't know which way to go. Whales don't like loud sounds, so people banged on pipes and all kinds of other things to drive her in the right direction, so she could swim away to safety."

Roshni asked, "Could we do the same?"

"It's worth a try!" Connor grinned as an idea came to him. "Hey, remember when Kiki got us all to do karaoke in the Exploration Station that time?"

Roshni rolled her eyes. "How could I forget?"

Connor leaned over the console. "Hey, Beagle? Can you fire up your speakers and microphone, please?"

A panel popped open and a microphone slid out.

Connor pulled open the supplies compartment. "Grab anything you can make a noise with."

Moments later, they were armed with a metal First Aid kit, some screw drivers and wrenches, a piece of copper tubing, and a safety helmet. They were ready to make the most horrendous racket they could.

They needed to nudge the whales south, so Connor steered the Beagle around the pod to the north. That way, when all the humpback whales swam away from the noise, they'd be heading in the right direction.

"Ready?" Connor said. "And a one, two, three, four..."

BANG! CRASH! CLANG! SKADOING!

The Beagle's cockpit rang with the din. Connor and Roshni made as much noise as they could, battering the helmet with the copper tube and clashing the tools together. The speakers broadcast the dreadful sounds into the sea all around.

One of the whales twitched a fin, but that was all.

"We need more noise!" Connor yelled. "Beagle, give me a beat!"

Instantly, the Beagle boomed out a rhythm. Roshni joined in, making beatbox noises. Connor grabbed the microphone and belted out a rap, making up the lyrics as he went along:

"It's time for you to move along! It's time for you to bail, whale!

You got another place to be! Come on and move your tail, whale!

You know you're going way too slow, so please don't be a snail, whale!

It's time for your migration and we need you not to fail, whale!"

Slowly but surely, the whales began to turn.

"It's working!" Connor cried out.

"I'm not surprised," Roshni joked. "That has to be the worst rapping I've ever heard in my life. I think I cringed my way into a parallel universe!"

They followed the pod to make sure the whales were really on the right course. Connor let himself relax a little. The whales would be okay now. He could just sit back and watch them swim. Now that he had the time to count them, he did—there were eighteen adults and three calves.

Roshni pointed. "That one's swimming up to the surface. Is it okay?"

"It's fine!" Connor told her. "Whales aren't fish. They're mammals, like us, so they breathe air, not water. To do that, they go up to the surface every few minutes."

"So how do they breathe, then?" Roshni asked.

"Through blowholes on the tops of their heads," Connor explained. "They're like big nostrils."

Roshni took a breath, held it as long as she could, and then gasped for air. "I don't think I'd make a very good whale," she wheezed.

Connor chuckled. "An adult humpback whale can last up to *forty-five minutes* between breaths. Can you imagine?"

"That's incredible," Roshni said. "Listen, they're singing again!"

The haunting sound of whale song rippled through the water. Roshni listened to it for a moment, her face frozen in wonder. Then she looked thoughtful, pressed some buttons on the Beagle's console and opened an instrument panel.

"What are you doing?" Connor asked.

"Recording the whale song," Roshni replied. "It's so beautiful, I want to listen to it when we're back on land."

Connor laughed. "Okay, I admit it. They're better singers than I am!"

Roshni glanced from her recording equipment over to the sonar screen. "Hey, look. There's a whole bunch of signals up on the surface, moving around. Could it be another pod of whales?"

Connor frowned. "Maybe. We'd better go up and have a look."

He gunned the engines and steered the Beagle to the surface. When they bobbed up, Connor was startled. They were much closer to Australia than he'd realized. He could clearly see land on the horizon—and the reason for the sonar signals...

Boats!

There were dozens of them on the water. Some had sails, some had motors, and they were all zipping along.

Roshni said, "The whales are going to need to come up for air, aren't they? What if they come up under those boats?"

"It would be very bad news," said Connor seriously. "We need to get the pod safely past these boats. Roshni, our mission's not over yet!"

Chapter Four
BOATS AHOY!

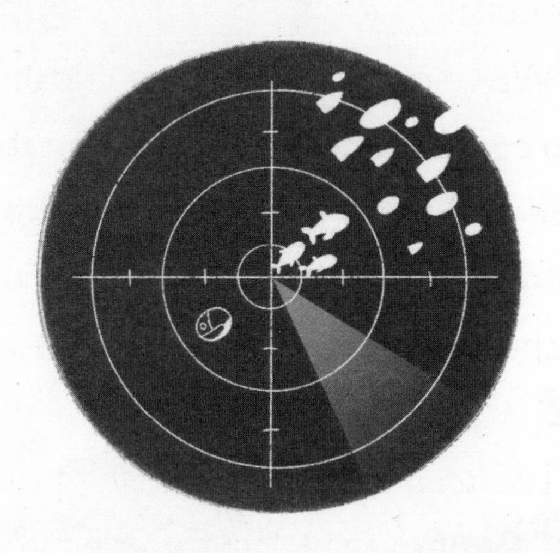

The sonar screen showed more dots than Connor and Roshni could count. Every single one was a boat—and they were heading right into the whales' path.

"So many boats! Is it a race or something?" Roshni asked, looking worried.

"It's just regular marine traffic," said Connor. "People going out fishing and having fun. And not one of them knows a pod of whales is about to swim right under their hulls!"

"We've got to warn them," Roshni said. "I'll try to contact one of the boats on the radio."

She flicked a switch on the Beagle's communications equipment. But the Beagle switched it back off again, with a warning **BUZZ**.

"Looks like the Beagle isn't happy about that," Connor said. "Wonder why?"

Roshni snapped her fingers. "Of course. We're the *Secret* Explorers—and we're supposed to stay secret! If we call those boats on our radio, they'll want to know who we are and what we're doing here."

"Maybe there's another way." Connor thought hard. "Beagle, can you zoom in on that yacht over there?"

The yacht was floating not far from where the Beagle bobbed on the surface. A close-up appeared on the screen, showing white sails and a sleek hull. The name *Enchantress* was written down the yacht's side.

On the deck was a boy about their age. He was wearing swim trunks and watching something intently. Had he spotted the Beagle? No—he was looking at a school of flying fish! They came leaping out of the water in glittering arcs. Their bodies flashed silver in the warm evening sunlight.

Connor was glad to see someone else who was interested in the ocean. "Maybe that boy can help," he said.

Connor submerged the Beagle just below the water. He and Roshni took the wet suits out of the storage cupboard and put them on, along with masks, oxygen tanks, and flippers.

Then he opened up a hatch in the floor, revealing water beneath. Connor climbed down first, lowering himself into the ocean. Roshni followed behind him. They swam away from the Beagle toward the pale hull of the *Enchantress.*

Connor surfaced right alongside the yacht. The boy was still watching the ocean, and he gave a surprised yelp as Connor and then Roshni appeared.

Connor waved up to him. "Hey! Mind if we come aboard?"

The boy gave them a wide grin. "Yeah, no worries!"

Roshni reached up and the boy helped her climb onto the deck, then did the same for Connor.

"I'm Jack," he said. "I've come out with my parents to do a bit of whale watching. But there are no whales so far today."

"Whales are exactly why we're here!" Connor said. "There's a pod of humpback whales swimming this way, but all these fast boats could be dangerous for them."

"No way!" Jack exclaimed.

Connor said, "There's still time to save them. We just need to clear all these boats out of their path. Can you signal to them to move?"

"You just watch me, mate," Jack said excitedly. "I'll get my parents to call the coastguard. When you hear the horn, it means we're on the move!" He ran over to the cabin door and shouted, "Mom? Dad? It's an emergency!"

"We'd better get out of here," Roshni whispered to Connor.

Connor nodded. "Thanks a million, Jack! Good luck!"

Before Jack's parents could appear, Connor and Roshni flipped backward off the deck and plunged into the water. They swam back to the Beagle as fast as they could. Soon they were climbing back up through the hatch, peeling off their wet suits and turning back to the controls.

Connor checked the sonar. His heart pounded. The whales were swimming right under the boats! If one of them surfaced now, it would mean disaster.

"Come on, Jack," he muttered. "Don't let us down..."

A long horn-blast rang out across the water.

"There's the signal!" Roshni cried.

Connor checked the periscope.

"The boats are moving. They're all heading back toward the shore!"

Roshni clapped her hands. "Jack's done it!"

Connor brought the Beagle back to the surface so they could watch what was happening. Sure enough, the boats were all sailing out of the whales' path. He caught a glimpse of Jack standing on the deck of the *Enchantress*, looking at the water again. Suddenly, a humpback whale came up to the surface and blew!

A great cheer went up from Jack and the other people watching from the boats. Another whale came up, and then another. Connor smiled to himself. The pod was safe!

"Let's get back to the whales," he said. "I want to make sure they're all okay."

He submerged the Beagle once more. But as they closed in on the whales, Connor saw to his dismay that the pod was off course again. Instead of heading south, the whales were now swimming east!

"The boats must have upset them so much they turned all the way around," he said with a groan. "We're right back where we started!"

"Actually, I think it's worse," Roshni said in a hollow voice.

"What? How?" Connor asked.

Roshni pointed. "How many calves did the whales have before?"

"Three," said Connor.

All eighteen of the adult whales were still there, swimming ahead. But Connor could only see two calves.

"They've lost one!" he said. "But if all the mothers are still here..."

"... then wherever that poor calf is, it's all alone," Roshni finished. "Connor, we've got to find it!"

Chapter Five
DEEP, DARK WATERS

The rest of the pod was already moving on. Connor wished he could call out to them. ***Turn around! You've left a calf behind!***

"We'll have to backtrack," he said. "Maybe the calf is swimming behind the rest of the pod."

He steered the Beagle back the way they had come. Meanwhile, Roshni carefully watched the sonar screen for any sign of the lost calf. Connor kept the Beagle just under the water's surface, so they could use the periscope. The calf might come up to breathe, and then they'd spot it.

"Poor little thing," Roshni murmured. "Don't worry, baby whale. We're coming to find you."

Connor said, "It may be a baby, but it's about 20 feet long! We ought to see it soon."

Roshni bent over the sonar screen. Connor peered out through the Beagle's windows. He saw darting fish and scraps of seaweed tumbling past, but no whale calf. To make matters worse, the sun was setting and the sea was growing darker. Soon it would be too dark to see without lights.

Suddenly, the Beagle pitched sideways and a horrific sound of scraping metal ripped through the cabin. Then came a sharp snapping noise. Something fell through the water past the window, trailing bubbles. The Beagle let out a babble of panicked bleeps. Roshni yelled and looked up from the screen. "What happened?"

"We've hit something!" Connor grabbed the controls and brought the Beagle down, away from the surface. He smacked his forehead with his palm. "I was looking out of the window, you were checking the sonar—and neither of us was steering! Sorry, Beagle."

The Beagle made a mournful noise, like a whining dog. Connor felt terrible.

He looked up at the hull of the boat they'd clipped, dreading what he might see. To his relief, it wasn't holed. That could have been a total disaster. Imagine sinking a boat *and* losing a whale calf...

"I think we might be okay," he said. "We took a nasty knock, but nothing's broken, right?"

Roshni winced and showed him the sonar screen. It was completely blank.

With growing alarm, Connor checked the rest of the Beagle's instruments. The screens had gone dark on a whole row of panels.

"We've lost all our navigation systems," he said. "But how?"

Roshni said, "Remember that snapping noise? And the thing that fell past the window? I think that was the navigation module. It must have broken off completely when we hit the boat."

Connor felt cold horror creeping through his whole body. Without the Beagle's special navigation module, they couldn't work the sonar or the satnav system. He was counting on that to find the missing calf. And even if they found the calf without it, how on earth would they find the rest of the pod?

"We've got to get it back!" he said.

He tilted the Beagle's nose until it was pointing downward, then fired the engines. They churned up the water and the Beagle shot down into the darkness. The controls vibrated in Connor's hands, but he held the sub steady. ***No more collisions***, he promised himself.

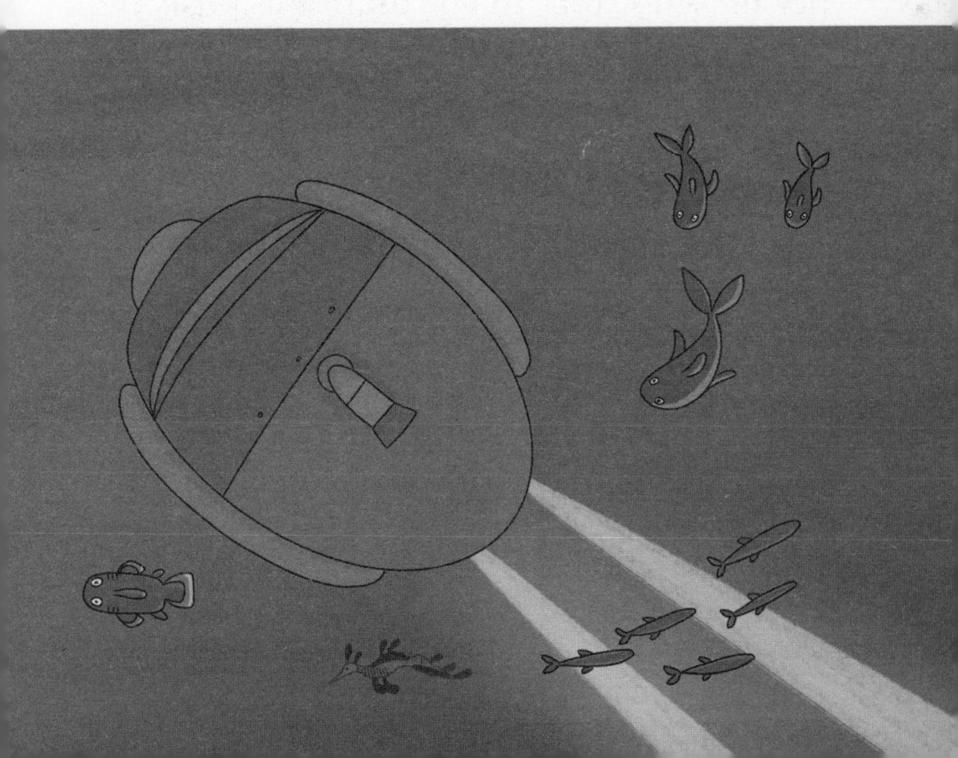

"I can see it!" cried Roshni.

Sure enough, the broken-off navigation module was ahead of them, turning over and over as it fell through the water. It looked like half a soccer ball, with wires and cables hanging out from it. Connor winced as he remembered seeing it attached to the top of the cockpit. He hoped they'd be able to reattach it.

The next moment it vanished from sight, swallowed up in the darkness. The water outside the sub was as black as the bottom of a well.

The Beagle made a serious-sounding **BLEEEEP**. Connor knew that the deeper they dived, the higher the water pressure. Now it would be closing on the Beagle like a clenching fist. At the same time, it was getting colder and colder.

Connor shivered.

He checked the depth gauge and saw they were nearly at the bottom of the ocean. Connor slowed the Beagle to a stop and looked around.

"Shouldn't we turn on the headlights?" asked Roshni.

"Not yet," Connor said. "Look."

Strange lights were glowing in the darkness. Roshni stared at them. "What are they?"

"That one there is an Atolla jellyfish," Connor said, pointing out a blue flashing light. "It flashes when it's under attack. And that steady glow? That's an angler fish. The light lures smaller fish in, so it can eat them."

"I've never seen anything like it," Roshni said.

Connor switched the headlights on and lit up the angler fish's whole body. Beneath the pretty light was a ghoulish face and a mouth full of pointed teeth! Roshni shuddered.

"The light's called bioluminescence," Connor explained. "It's created by a chemical reaction."

"Wow!" Roshni glanced up at a billowy shape that was drifting by overhead. "What's that one?"

Connor wasn't sure what the pale creature might be. "Some kind of jellyfish, I think. It's coming this way."

Roshni's face fell. "Oh, dear. I think this is a member of the species *plasticus baggus*."

Connor grimaced in disgust. "Yeah," he said. The mysterious "jellyfish" was nothing but a supermarket plastic bag, swept along by the undersea currents. It sickened him to think of plastic pollution down here among these wonderful ocean creatures.

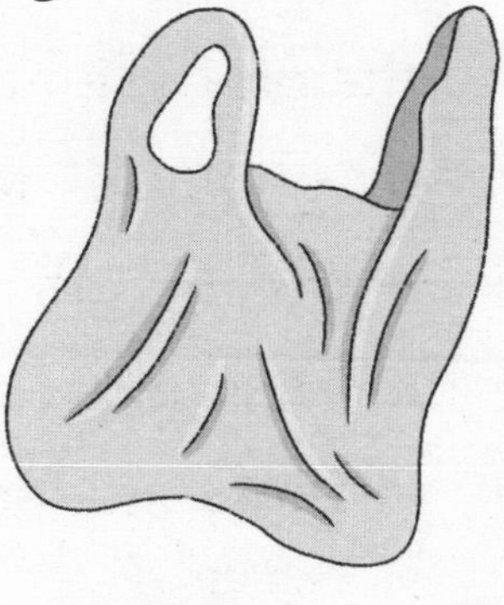

Roshi said, "I'll swim out and get it."

She went to put her wet suit back on, but Connor quickly stopped her. "No!"

"What's wrong?"

Connor pointed out the water pressure gauge. "We can't go out there. At this depth, the pressure would crush us!"

But they couldn't just leave the plastic bag on the ocean floor. They began exploring the Beagle's cockpit, in the hope of finding something that might help.

"Aha!" Connor said. "The grabber arm! We can use that!"

He found the switch and turned it on. A long robotic arm slid out from the Beagle's underside. Connor moved it back and forth and tested the grabber.

"How is it?" Roshni asked.

"Easier to use than the claw machines at the arcade," Connor joked.

As the plastic bag drifted back in their direction, Connor used the robotic arm to quickly snatch it up. The Beagle helpfully opened up a storage compartment and Connor stowed the bag inside.

"Scientists use arms just like this on research subs," he told Roshni. "They can take samples from the seabed or recover items from sunken ships!"

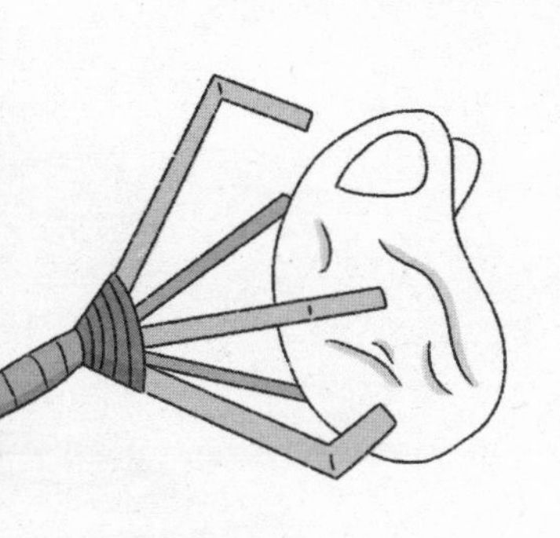

"And we can use it to get the navigation module back!" Roshni burst out.

"Brilliant idea," Connor said. "But... where is it?"

In the excitement of seeing the luminous sea creatures, they'd lost track of the module. Now they couldn't see it anywhere.

Connor's stomach tightened into a knot. If they didn't find the module it would pollute the water, just like the plastic bag.

"We've got to find it," Connor said. "If we don't, we'll never find the calf and the rest of the whale pod!"

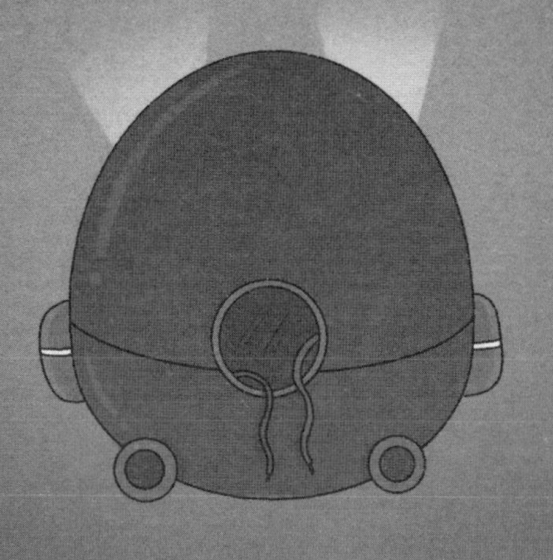

Chapter Six
UNDER PRESSURE

Connor adjusted the Beagle's headlights until they were pointing down at the seabed. Then he set the Beagle so it would move automatically in a circle around where the module had fallen. That way, they would have the best chance of spotting it.

"Do you see it yet?" he asked Roshni.

"Not yet," she said.

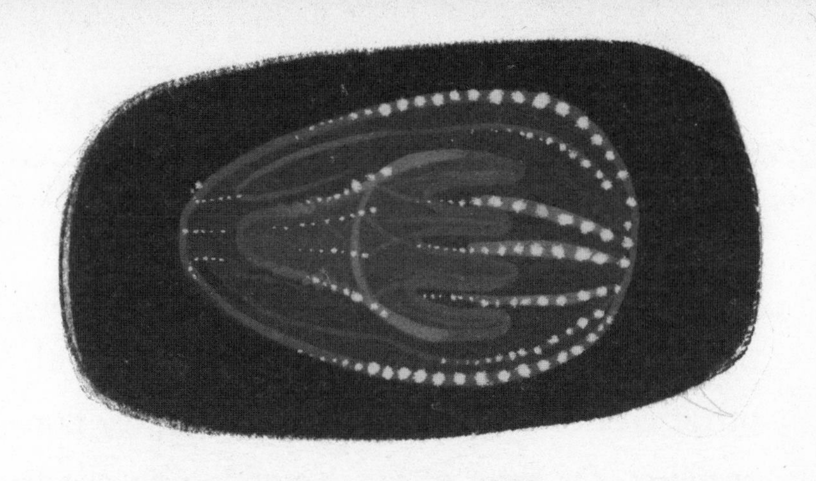

"Come on," Connor said through gritted teeth. "Where is it?"

Above them, in the darkness, rainbow light glimmered.

Roshni gasped. "What's that?"

Connor recognized it at once. "It's a real jellyfish this time! It's called a comb jelly. Another bioluminescent species."

"It's pretty!" said Roshni. "It looks like it's covered in tiny stars."

The jellyfish was about 18 inches long. It floated above their heads, bright twinkles sparkling on its transparent body.

"Why do the creatures down here glow?" Roshni asked.

"Lots of reasons," Connor said. "Scientists think it might be a way to communicate with other creatures, or to lure prey so they can catch it. Or they might be trying to scare away rivals."

"But there aren't any other creatures here," Roshni said thoughtfully. "Unless..."

She grabbed the headlight control and swiveled the beams of light in the direction the comb jelly had come from.

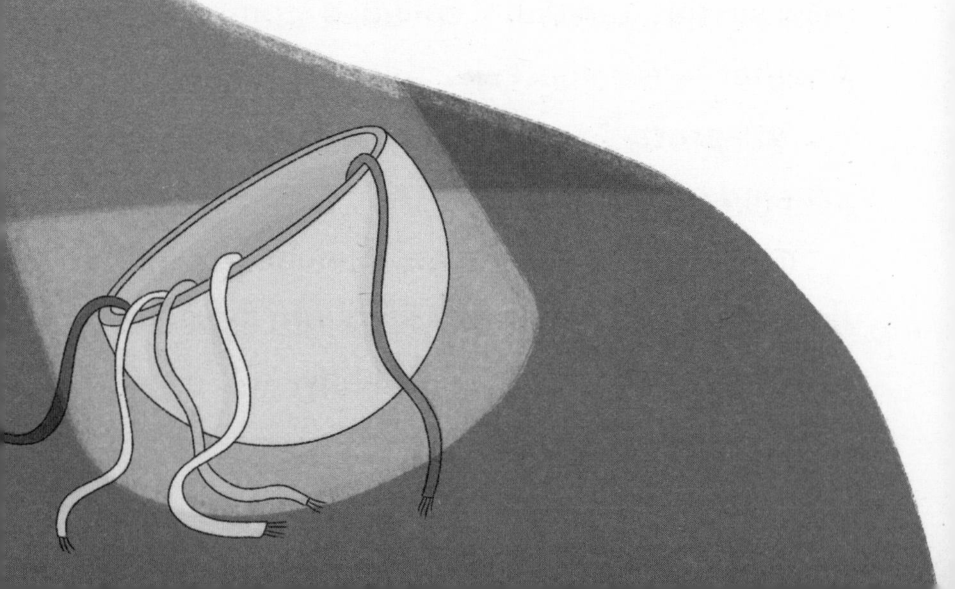

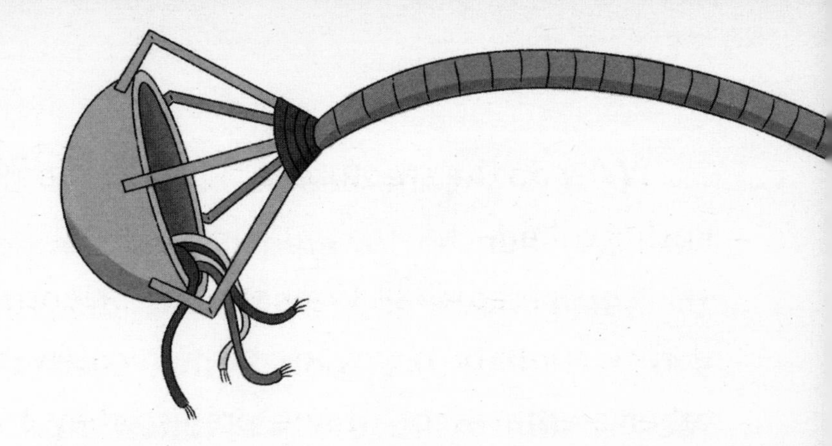

There, wedged in an outcrop of undersea rock, was the missing navigation module!

"Maybe the jelly thought the module was another creature!" Connor exclaimed.

"Thanks, little guy," Roshni called back at the departing jelly.

Connor extended the robotic arm, took hold of the navigation module and stowed it safely in the storage compartment. The Beagle let out a long beep that sounded a lot like "Phew!"

Connor felt relieved, too. Now they could get back to their mission! He just hoped it wasn't too late for the lost whale calf.

He brought the Beagle back up to the surface. Then he lowered himself through the hatch and climbed up the outside of the sub and onto the roof. Roshni used the robotic arm to lift the navigation module back into place. Connor did his best to reconnect all the wires and cables, but engineering wasn't his specialty subject. Sparks shot out, and the Beagle made an unhappy ***EEP!***

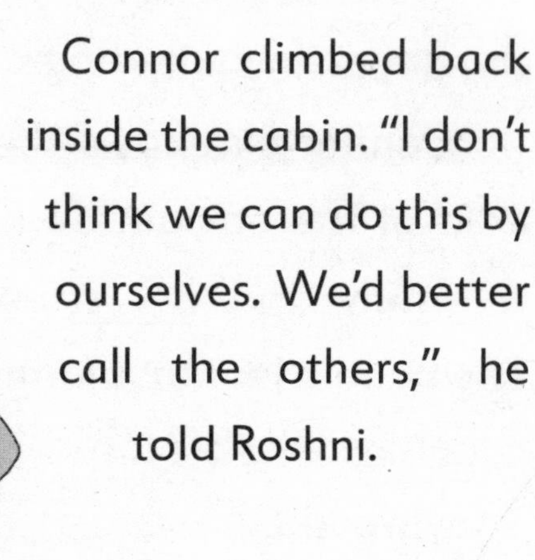

Connor climbed back inside the cabin. "I don't think we can do this by ourselves. We'd better call the others," he told Roshni.

Roshni switched on the communications panel. "Beagle calling Exploration Station! We need help!"

An image of the Exploration Station appeared on the screen, showing all the other Secret Explorers at their computers. They waved.

"We've all been watching your mission on our monitors!" Leah said.

"Yeah!" said Cheng with a grin. "You're doing brilliantly!"

"Do you think the whales are going to be okay?" Tamiko asked nervously.

"I'm sure we can still help them," Connor assured her. "But we need to fix the Beagle. And quick. Kiki, you're the Engineering Explorer. Can you talk us through the repairs?"

"Show me the damage," Kiki said.

Connor held the broken module up to the screen.

Kiki sucked air through her teeth. "Yeesh! You two really did a number on that module, didn't you? I couldn't fix that without my special workbench, guys. I'm sorry."

"Thanks anyway, Kiki," Connor said. "We'll figure something out."

"Good luck! We're all rooting for you here," said Gustavo.

The other Secret Explorers waved goodbye. Connor and Roshni waved, too, and shut the communicator off. The two of them shared a worried glance.

"So what are we supposed to do now?" Roshni asked.

Connor pressed his knuckles to his forehead and thought as hard as he could. The lost calf was nowhere to be seen. Nor was the rest of the pod. Worse still, the sun had almost vanished behind the western horizon. Without either the sun or the navigation module to help them, they couldn't tell which way was south. So they couldn't help the whales get back on the right course.

Maybe I should try thinking like a whale, he thought to himself.

How did whales find their way around their underwater world? They used sonar, but they didn't have electric equipment. They made their own sound waves and bounced them off objects. Dolphins did it, too, and it was how bats navigated through the night sky.

Maybe sound was the answer...

"I wonder if we could use sound to find the missing calf," he said.

"I'm not sure," Roshni said. "You don't want to scare the calf away with your terrible rapping, do you?"

Connor sighed. "Yeah. It was a silly idea. If I could sing like a whale, maybe things would be different..."

He froze. An idea had just lit up like a light bulb inside his mind.

"Why didn't I think of this before? We *can* sing like a whale!" he yelled. "Roshni, you're a genius!"

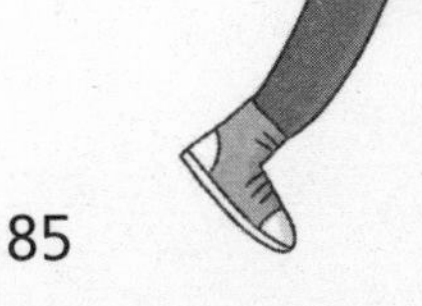

Roshni looked puzzled. "I am? Thanks, I guess! But what did I do?"

Connor used the Beagle's console to find the sound file Roshni had made earlier. "You recorded the whale song, remember? We can play it through the speakers!"

Roshni's face brightened. "Will that bring the lost calf over to us?"

"I don't know, but I really hope so," Connor said. "Because I think it's our last chance!"

Chapter Seven

WHALE SONG

Roshni switched the microphone and speakers back on. Connor clicked the "PLAY" button and the whale song began. It swelled out from the sub, echoing far into the dark and lonely depths.

They looked around hopefully. Connor felt a rush of excitement as he saw something swimming toward them, about the right size to be the calf. But then it turned sideways to pass them, and he saw the long spike protruding from its nose. It was a swordfish! Any other time, he'd have been overjoyed to see it.

The whale song stopped. He quickly clicked the "PLAY" button again.

Connor chewed his lip anxiously as they peered into the shadows. But there was nothing but swirling sediment and tiny fish. The whale song ended again. He crossed his fingers for luck and played it one more time.

Then, out of nowhere, a shape appeared. A humpbacked shape 20 feet long and swimming curiously toward them...

Connor was about to yell, "It's the calf!" But, just in time, he remembered the microphone was still on! He tapped Roshni's shoulder and put his finger to his lips. Her eyes widened as she saw it.

Connor tried to imagine what the calf was thinking. What could this strange thing be, which sounded like a whale but wasn't one and was all lit up with bright and shiny lights?

The calf swam around the Beagle. Roshni put her hand up to the window pane, just as

the calf pressed against it.

"It's like I'm touching it!" she whispered.

Connor watched the calf in amazement. It turned around to face him. For one instant he looked right into its eye, and a thrill went through his whole body. He had never been this close to such an astonishing creature.

The calf gazed at Connor, and Connor looked back at it. It didn't look afraid, and he was deeply glad of that. Then, without warning, it rolled all the way over.

"What's it doing?" Roshni asked.

The calf lashed its tail, looked at them, and rolled over again. Strange clicking noises came from it. Connor recognized the funny noises as whale language.

"It's trying to play with us!" he said, and laughed in delight. "The calf knows the Beagle is a friend."

The Beagle made a joyful ***SQUEAK*** through its console. The calf heard it through the speakers and let loose a series of happy clicks in response.

Then, from somewhere close by, more whale song came booming through the water.

"Could that be the mother whale, calling for her calf?" asked Roshni.

"It's not just one whale," Connor replied. "Look at that!"

Suddenly, enormous whales loomed all around them!

The entire pod had answered their call. A chorus of whale song greeted the lost calf, welcoming it back. The Beagle seemed very tiny next to these magnificent creatures.

Roshni gave Connor a hug. "I'm glad you got to see this," she said. "I know how much you love the oceans."

He grinned and hugged her back. "Look at them! They're not scared of us at all.

I think... maybe they understand what we've been trying to do."

They watched the whales swim around them for a moment and listened to their uncanny song.

Roshni pointed. "Connor, look!" The calf and its mother had found one another again. They were swimming close together, side by side. Humpback whales can't smile, but Connor was sure those two would if they could.

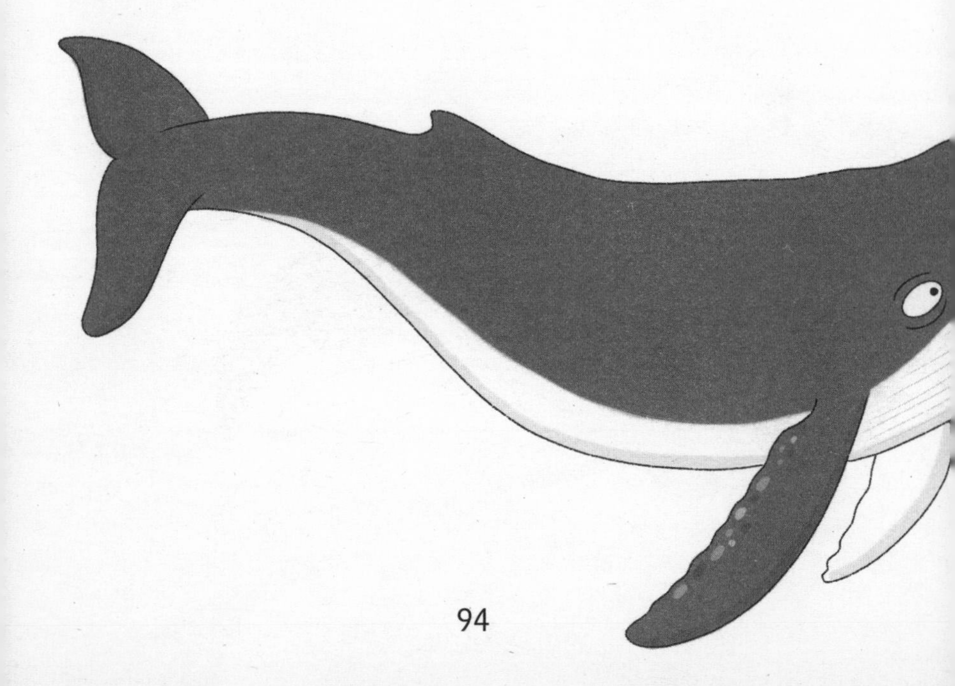

They certainly looked happy to be reunited.

He and Roshni cheered and high-fived one another.

"We still need to get the pod back on its correct migration course," Connor said.

Roshni nodded. "Which means heading south."

"But how? The sun's gone down, and we couldn't fix the navigation module."

Connor looked out at the pod and hoped he hadn't let the whales down after all.

Roshni pondered for a moment.

"It might not matter that the sun's gone down. Remember what I said about the comb jelly?"

Connor thought back. "You said its body looked like it was covered in stars."

"Right! And that's given me an idea. The sun might be down, but the stars will be out, won't they? If I can find the right constellations, I can navigate by the stars!"

"Of course!" Connor said. "Sailors have used stars to find their way for thousands of years," Roshni said.

"But you're the Space Explorer – I thought you wanted to be an astronaut, not a sailor?" Connor joked.

"Where do you think the word 'astronaut' comes from?" Roshni said with a grin." *Astron* means star, and *nautes* means sailor. Astronauts are literally star sailors!"

Connor brought the Beagle up to the surface. The night sky was filled with stars. Roshni looked up and searched the sky.

"There!" she cried out, pointing to a group of four stars. "Do you see it, Connor? The Southern Cross!"

"Yeah," Connor said. Those stars were so bright, he could hardly have missed them. They stood out like jewels on a black cloth.

Roshni frowned in concentration. "Here's what you do. Draw an imaginary line from the top star through to the bottom. Then keep the line going for four and a half times that length."

"Got it," Connor said, picturing the line in his mind.

"Great! Now drop another line straight down from the end of the first line. Where it hits the horizon marks due south!"

Connor could hardly believe it. "It's really that easy?"

Roshni laughed. "It is when you know how!"

Connor set the whale song playing again, while Roshni steered the Beagle south. With any luck, the whales would follow the song.

Connor didn't need to worry. The whales seemed to know what they were doing. They followed along behind the sub, answering the whale song he was playing with a song of their own.

"Funny to think that we dove deep under the sea, but the answer was in the stars all along," Roshni said happily.

"I guess now we know why the Space Explorer got sent on an underwater mission," Connor said with a grin. "I'm really glad you're here, Roshni!"

Chapter Eight

HEADING HOME

The farther south they went, the colder the waters became. Connor knew they must be well on their way to Antarctica.

After the Beagle had guided the pod of whales south for a while, all at once they suddenly began to swim much faster. A new, excited mood seemed to have come over them. They swam right past the Beagle and kept going.

"What's happening? Are the whales okay?" asked Roshni.

"They're fine, I think," Connor replied. "They must recognize where they are. They're back on their migration route!"

One by one, the whales overtook them. Last of all came the mother whale and the calf they'd rescued, who was swimming right beside her. The mother whale broke away from the others and began swimming up to the surface.

Roshni and Connor traded glances. Without saying a word, Connor guided the Beagle after her. He kept the sub a safe distance away.

They reached the surface first and looked out over the glittering dark waters.

"What's she doing?" Roshni asked.

"Just watch," Connor whispered.

The whale launched herself out of the water. Time seemed to slow down as her enormous body rose, turned and fell. She came crashing down onto her back, sending foam and water up

in a massive burst. The Beagle rocked around crazily.

Moments later, the little calf flung itself out of the water, copying what its mother had done. It made a much smaller splash, but Connor and Roshni still clapped and cheered!

One by one, the other whales rose, too. They blew jets of spray from their blowholes, then dived back down again.

"I think they're saying goodbye," Roshni said.

Connor nodded. "Goodbye," he called out to them. "I'll never forget this."

The last of the whales vanished below the surf. The flukes that flared out at the end of its huge tail flicked for a moment, like a vast waving hand. Then it was gone.

"They'll be okay from here, right?" Roshni asked.

"More than okay," Connor replied. "They'll find their way to the Antarctic just fine. They don't need our help anymore."

With a soft ***PING***, the "START" button on the Beagle's dashboard lit up. Now it read "HOME." Connor and Roshni breathed a sigh of relief. "Mission accomplished," Roshni said. "Let's go!"

Connor pushed the button.

The Beagle shuddered and trembled, as if it were going through a car wash. The engines behind them gave a deafening roar. Suddenly, like they were being shot from a massive rubber band, the Beagle rushed forward at mindboggling speed. They were whizzing through a tunnel of dazzling white light.

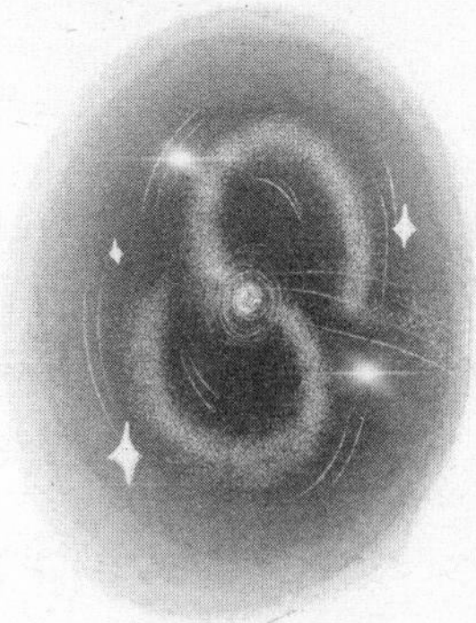

Around them, the Beagle's cockpit began to change. The dashboard sank back into the floor, the glass bubble slid backward and vanished, the padded seats deflated like an air bed, all the compartments and equipment folded away like a magic trick, and four

rather wobbly-looking wheels appeared on the corners. Once more, the Beagle was nothing but a shabby old go-kart... with a lot of secrets.

The white light faded away. The Beagle was standing on its platform in the middle of the Exploration Station. Feeling a little dizzy, Connor and Roshni climbed out of the seats.

All the other Secret Explorers jumped up from their computer chairs and came sprinting over. They gathered excitedly around Connor and Roshni.

"That was amazing!" Cheng said. "All those undersea rock formations!"

"And the different kinds of seaweed!" Leah said.

"What was it like when the whale breached?" asked Gustavo.

"You guys did an amazing job," Ollie said. "I'm so glad the whales are safe."

Connor and Roshni sat on the big padded sofas, had some cold drinks, and talked all about their mission. All the Secret Explorers agreed it had been a spectacular success.

"Hey, Kiki," Connor said, "do you think you can fix the damage to the Beagle? Whoever takes it out on the next mission is going to need that navigation module."

"No problem!" Kiki grinned. "The Beagle is always getting into scrapes. I'll patch it right up."

Leah went and opened the display cabinets. "Did you bring anything back for the collection?"

Connor took a thumb drive out of his pocket. He'd copied the whale song recording on to it earlier.

"You're going to want to listen to this."

He played the sound file through the Exploration Station speakers.

When the Secret Explorers heard the strange sounds echoing around the room, their faces filled with awe. No one said a word. They all looked up at the domed ceiling, where the map of the night sky was, and listened to the unearthly music of the whales.

Afterward, Connor put the thumb drive in the display case between a piece of black volcanic glass that Cheng had collected and a bonsai tree that Leah had brought from Japan.

It was time to go home. "Bye, Roshni," Connor said. "Bye, everyone! See you on the next mission!"

Everyone waved and called out their goodbyes. Connor headed over to the glowing door he'd come in by, and stepped back through it.

A raging wind whipped through his hair and ruffled his clothes. White light roared up around him and faded away just as quickly. Seconds later, he found himself standing in his kitchen.

He glanced back over his shoulder. The pantry was just a pantry. There were cereal boxes, cans of beans, a bag of potatoes—nothing at all out of the ordinary. Nothing to show that anything exciting had ever happened here.

Connor could almost believe that he'd dreamed the whole adventure. But he knew he hadn't. No time at all had passed back here at home, but he'd been gone for several hours, and now he was hungry.

He reached up and took a granola bar from the shelf and headed outside to eat it. He crouched down beside the pond, unwrapped the bar, and took a bite.

Down in the pond, the toad tadpoles were peacefully swimming in their shoals. They looked like they were enjoying the clear water.

Connor grinned to see them. Swimming together like that, they reminded him of the pod of whales. He'd keep on looking out for the tadpoles, just as he had for the pod. And though he couldn't just scoop the red tide out of the ocean as easily as he'd scooped the green algae out of his own little pond, he could still do his part to help keep the seas clean.

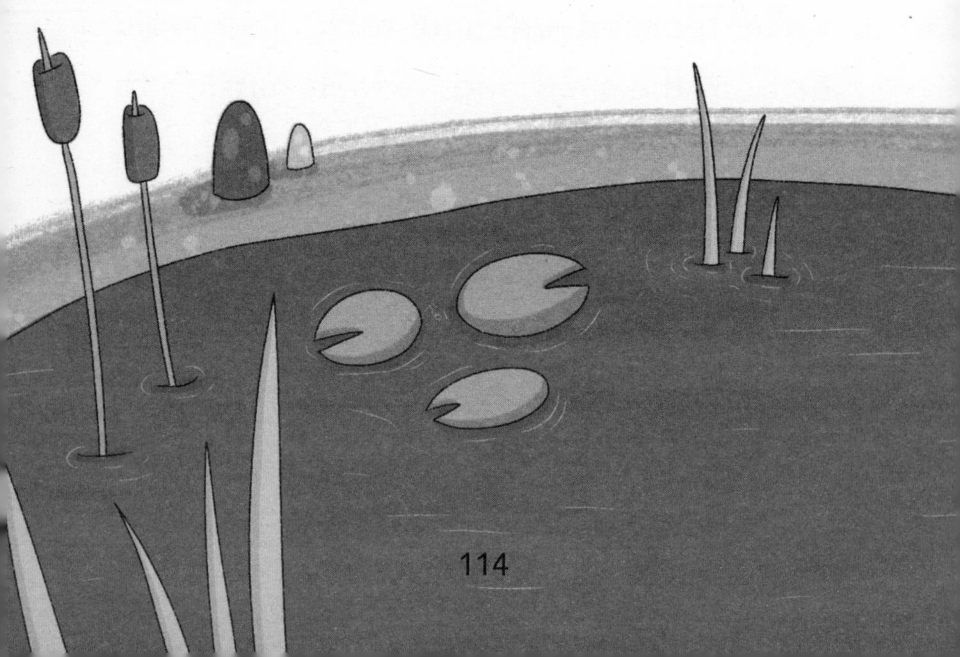

Connor loved being a Secret Explorer. This mission had been one of the best yet. And he couldn't wait to go on the next one!

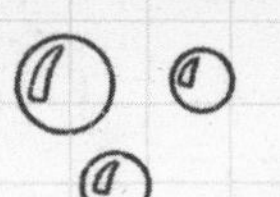

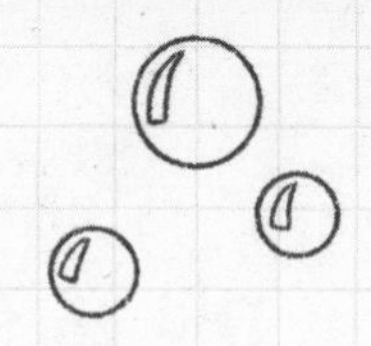

CONNOR'S

MISSION NOTES

THE HUMPBACK WHALE

* **Latin name**: *Megaptera novaeangliae*
* **Animal type**: Mammals—they breathe air, have warm blood, and give birth to live young
* **Location**: Worldwide, but usually nearer coasts
* **Length**: Up to 56 ft (17 m)
* **Weight**: 37 tons (34 metric tons)—heavier than five African elephants!

In the southern oceans, humpback feed mainly on Antarctic krill.

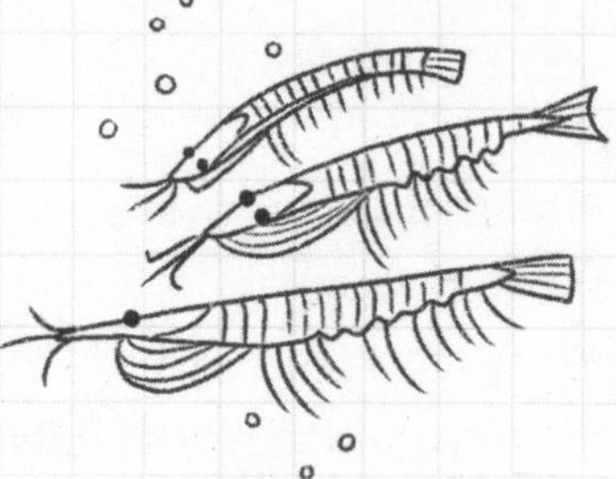

Each whale has a unique pattern on the underside of its tail.

The pectoral flippers of the humpback are one-third of its body length—longer than those of other whales.

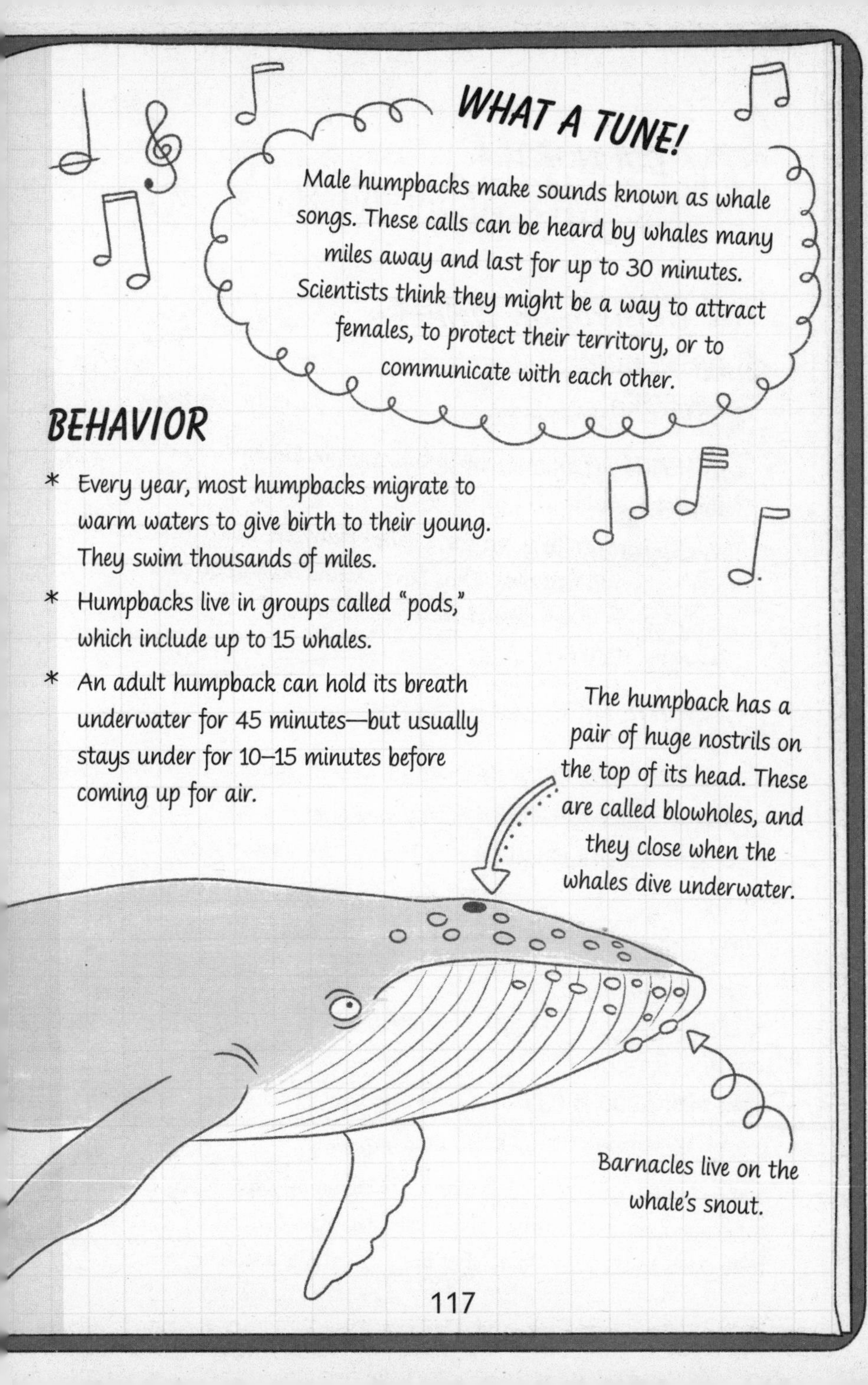

WHAT A TUNE!

Male humpbacks make sounds known as whale songs. These calls can be heard by whales many miles away and last for up to 30 minutes. Scientists think they might be a way to attract females, to protect their territory, or to communicate with each other.

BEHAVIOR

* Every year, most humpbacks migrate to warm waters to give birth to their young. They swim thousands of miles.
* Humpbacks live in groups called "pods," which include up to 15 whales.
* An adult humpback can hold its breath underwater for 45 minutes—but usually stays under for 10–15 minutes before coming up for air.

OCEAN LIFE

Sunlit zone

* Top 650 ft (200 m) of the ocean.
* Lots of different animals live in this zone, including humpback whales.
* It is also home to tiny creatures called plankton, which includes baby crabs and fish eggs. They float around on the currents. Many sea creatures depend on plankton for food.

Twilight zone

* From 650 ft to 3,300 ft (200 m to 1, 000 m) below the surface.
* The little sunlight that reaches this zone gives it a faint blue glow. Fewer animals live here than in the sunlit zone.
* Some areas of this zone don't have much oxygen, so the only animals that can live here have special adaptations.

Midnight zone

* More than 3,300 ft (1,000 m) down, no light at all reaches this zone.
* It is up to 33,000 ft (10,000 m) deep in places.
* Some of the creatures that live here are bioluminescent—they create their own light. For example, the anglerfish has a lure on top of its head that glows in the dark to attract prey—a bit like a fishing pole.

Dolphin
Reef fish
Turtle
Lantern fish
Comb jellyfish
Vampire squid
Anglerfish
Deep sea squid
Viperfish

OCEANS IN DANGER!

The Earth's climate is getting warmer—which is bad news for the oceans. Rising temperatures affect the life cycles of certain sea creatures, threatening their survival.

GLOBAL WARMING

Greenhouse gases, such as carbon dioxide and methane, build up in the atmosphere. This causes a greenhouse effect, as the gases stop heat from leaving the Earth's atmosphere—just like the glass windows that keep a greenhouse warm.

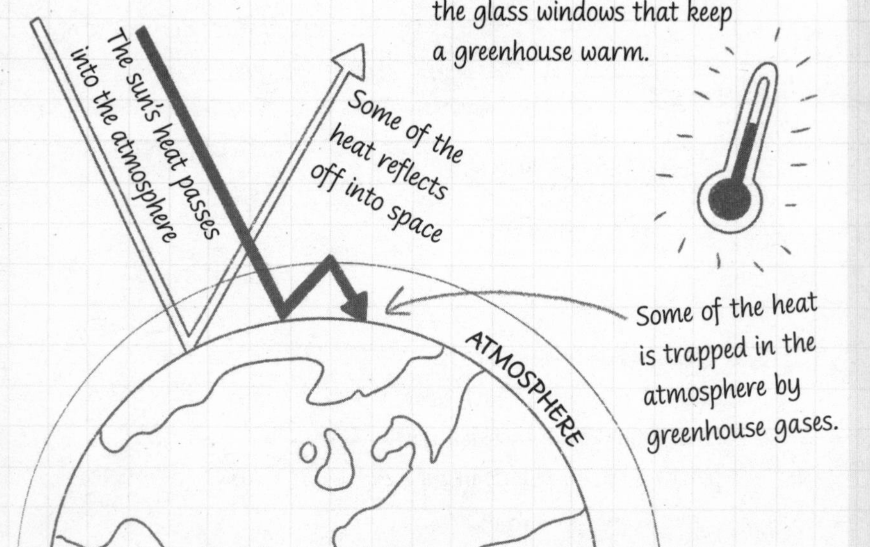

WHAT CAUSES IT?

* Burning fossil fuels such as coal, gas, and oil to generate electricity and power vehicles. When fossil fuels are burned, they release carbon dioxide into the atmosphere.
* Cutting down trees that absorb carbon dioxide. They are the world's best natural air filters!
* Cows' burping and farting releases lots of methane. In addition, forests are often cut down to clear land for them to graze.

THINGS THAT MAKE THE OCEAN SAD...

Warming seas and increased amounts of carbon dioxide and pollution in the water are destroying coral reefs. This leads to the loss of many fish and other animals.

Millions of tons of plastic end up in our oceans each year. Ocean animals can accidentally eat tiny bits of plastic in the water, or get caught in the garbage.

QUIZ

1. What is the name for a group of whales?

2. For how long can an adult humpback whale hold its breath underwater?

3. Which shark has a T-shaped head with eyes at the ends?

4. What do humpback whales eat?

5. What is a red tide made of?

6. Where would you find a humpback whale's blowholes?

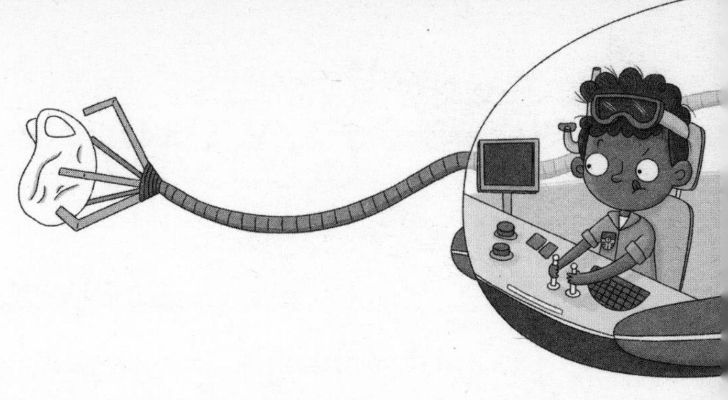

7 What do the Atolla jellyfish, the anglerfish, and the comb jelly all have in common?

8 What is a baby whale called?

FIND THE SEA DRAGONS!

Throughout the book we've hidden eight camouflaged sea dragons—can you find them?

They look like this!

Check your answers on page 127

GLOSSARY

ALGAE
a group of plant-like organisms, most of which live in water

ALGAL BLOOM
a rapid increase in the growth of algae

ASTRONAUT
a person who has been trained to travel into space

BARNACLE
a shelled sea creature that attaches itself tightly to rocks and other surfaces

BIOLUMINESCENCE
when a living organism produces its own light

CHARLES DARWIN
English naturalist who studied animals and plants

CONSTELLATION
a group of stars that form a pattern

FOSSIL FUELS
the remains of organisms that died millions of years ago that can be burned to release energy

GLOBAL WARMING
an increase in global temperature due to high greenhouse gas levels

GREENHOUSE GAS
a gas in the atmosphere that traps the sun's warmth around the planet, such as carbon dioxide and methane

HARBOR
a place on the coast where boats can dock

HORIZON
the line where the sky seems to meet the sea

KRILL

small shrimp-like animal eaten by many sea creatures, including whales

MARINE BIOLOGIST

someone who studies ocean life

MIGRATION

when animals make a long, regular journey from one place to another

POD

a name for a group of whales

POLLUTION

something harmful that gets into the air, a water source, or the soil

SCHOOL

a group of fish swimming together

SONAR

a system that locates things underwater or in the air using sound echoes

SUBMARINE
a ship designed to work underwater

TADPOLE
a young frog or toad

WATER PRESSURE
the amount of pressure exerted by water. Water pressure increases the deeper you dive

WET SUIT
a close-fitting piece of clothing worn while diving

Quiz answers

1. Pod
2. 45 minutes
3. Hammerhead
4. Krill
5. Algae
6. On top of its head
7. They are all bioluminescent (give off their own light)
8. Calf

Text for DK by Working Partners Ltd
9 Kingsway, London WC2B 6XF
With special thanks to Adrian Bott

Design by Collaborate Ltd
Illustrator Ellie O'Shea
Consultant Derek Harvey

Acquisitions Editor Sam Priddy
Senior Commissioning Designer Joanne Clark
US Editor Margaret Parrish
US Senior Editor Shannon Beatty
Senior Production Editor Nikoleta Parasaki
Senior Producer Ena Matagic
Publishing Director Sarah Larter

First American Edition, 2020
Published in the United States by DK Publishing
1450 Broadway, Suite 801 New York, New York 10018

20 21 22 23 24 10 9 8 7 6 5 4
004–318761–Jul/2020

Published in Great Britain by Dorling Kindersley Limited.

A catalog record for this book is available from the Library of Congress.

ISBN 978-0-7440-2105-9 (Paperback)
ISBN 978-0-7440-2384-8 (Hardcover)

Printed and bound in Great Britain by
Clays Ltd, Elcograf S.p.A.

The publisher would like to thank: Sally Beets and Seeta Parmar for editorial assistance; and Caroline Twomey for proofreading.